THE LION BOOK OF
Two-Minute
BEDTIME STORIES

Retold by Elena Pasquali
Illustrated by Nicola Smee

LION
CHILDREN'S

Contents

Go Fast Slowly

A STORY FROM THE PHILIPPINES

There's another

and another

"This is the best harvest ever!"

The farmer rubbed his hands with glee and set to work. He was gathering his crop of melons to take to market.

There were so many melons that the job took longer than expected. The sun was high in the sky as he set off in his donkey cart.

"I must hurry," he said to himself. "I shall take the track my neighbour uses as a short cut."

So when he came to the place, he turned off the road.

But the track was stonier than the road, so he could not go as fast. Nor could he turn round, for the track was narrow.

Then he came across a group of children who were out picking wild berries.

"Excuse me," he said. "Will it take me long to reach the road to town this way?"

I'm in a hurry

"It depends," said the eldest girl. "If you go slowly, it will take about ten minutes. If you go fast, it will take half an hour."

"What a foolish child," said the man to himself.
"She said the opposite of what she meant."

And with that, he shook the reins to make his
donkey go faster.

All at once, a wheel struck a large stone.
The jolt sent all the melons flying.

Oh no!

He had to stop and pick up all the melons. They had rolled this way and that and the job seemed to take for ever.

Can we help?

Then he saw the children. They were walking slowly so as not to lose a single berry from their baskets.

"Oh dear!" said the girl to the man. "You went so fast that the journey has taken you a whole hour."

Rabbit, Elephant, and Whale

A STORY FROM MAURITIUS

Rabbit was hippety-hopping through the forest, looking for something to do. Then he saw Elephant.

"Hello, Mr Elephant," he called. "I'm bored. Shall we go off on an adventure together?"

Elephant looked down and flapped his ears.

"I'm eating," he said huffily. "And I don't want to play silly rabbit games."

And with that, he turned away.

Rabbit went hippety-hopping down to the sea looking for something else to do.

terrump!

whooosh

Then he saw Whale.

"Hello, Mrs Whale," he called. "I'm bored. Shall we go off on an adventure together?"

Whale lifted her eye above the waves and blew noisily.

"I'm eating," she said huffily. "And what kind of games can a whale and a rabbit play?"

Rabbit sat down glumly. Then he had an idea.

"We can play Tug," he cried. "You take one end of this long vine, and then I go far away. When I say 'Go', you swim away from shore to see if you can get me wet."

"Oh, just the once then," sighed Whale.

And she took one end of the vine Rabbit flung her. Rabbit took the other end of the vine and scampered away to Elephant.

"I've got an idea!" he said. "We can play Tug with this vine.
I'll try to pull you down to the seashore."

Then Rabbit went and hid behind a rock and shouted, "Ready?"

Whale splashed as she swam as hard as she could.

Elephant strained and struggled for as long as he could.

"Do you give in?" cried Rabbit.

With a sigh, both Elephant and Whale let the vine go.

And from that day on, they were very respectful
to Rabbit.

oof

The Milkmaid and Her Pail

A STORY FROM AESOP

splish

The little milkmaid was going to market. On her head she carried a pail of creamy milk.

Beside her was her little brother.

"This milk is the best milk," she told him, "and I shall get a lot of money for it today."

The little boy looked up at his sister.

"What will you buy?" he asked.

Wow

cluck

At that moment a farmer went by, his cart loaded with things to sell.

"I shall by some of those chickens," she said, "and they will lay lots of eggs for me to sell."

"But who will buy them?" asked her brother.

At that moment a wealthy lady went by, riding daintily on a fine horse.

"I shall sell them to that lady," said the milkmaid. "She will pay a good price. I will save what I earn, and soon I shall have a whole purse of money."

"Then what will you buy?" asked her brother.

clip clop

15

The sister thought and thought, and soon they
had reached the first of the market stalls.

"I shall buy a fine dress from that stall,"
said the girl.

"And look at the milliner's: I shall buy
a fancy hat and trim it with ribbon."

"And then," she went on, "all the young men will turn their heads and notice me."

"And then all the other girls will be jealous of me!" she exclaimed. "But when they glare, I shall just toss my head like this."

As she spoke, she tossed her head and the pail fell off. And all the milk was spilt.

Oh

lap lap

The Wise Man and the Thief

Give me the money

A STORY FROM THE FAR EAST

The wise man who lived at the edge of the wood was in his garden, hoeing the weeds.

A thief came out of the shadows brandishing a sword.

"Your money or your life," he shouted.

The wise man looked up.

"I'm rather busy," he said.

"The money is in the drawer of the table."

Help yourself

18

The thief was rather startled by this, but even so he hurried inside and swept the coins into his purse.

The wise man came to the door.

"I meant to ask," he said, "if you would leave just one coin. I need it to pay the rent on my home."

The thief had never been stopped in the middle of a robbery before. Astonished, he tossed a coin onto the table and ran out.

"You forgot," called the wise man, "to thank me. That's not polite."

The thief stopped, feeling bewildered.

"Um… very kind of you, thank you very much," he said.

Excuse me!

Er… Thanks

A few days later, the town clerk came to visit the wise man. With him was a soldier, and the soldier had the thief in handcuffs.

"We have reason to believe," said the clerk, "that this man robbed you… as he has robbed others."

"Not me," said the wise man. "I gave him the money. He thanked me for it."

Because of what the wise man said, the thief did not spend too long in prison. While he was there, he felt sorry for all he had done. When he came out, he decided to change his ways.

Can you teach me about gardening?

The Nightingale

A STORY FROM HANS CHRISTIAN ANDERSEN

The emperor of China stood in the
moonlight and listened to the nightingale.
Then he clapped his hands with delight.
"What a joyful melody," he said to his servants.
   "Bring the bird to my palace. It will live in a golden cage
and sing to me when I am sad."

Now, the nightingale had been chosen among the birds to chase away bad dreams and sad thoughts. It agreed to come to the palace, and every evening it sang.

trill trill

The emperor was happier than he had ever been.

The servants were happier than they had ever been.

The emperor's daughter was the happiest of all.

meep

Poor nightingale

But as time went by, the nightingale began to long for the silver moon and the cool night breeze and the shadows of the dark woods… and the one who could chase away sadness itself grew sad.

23

tinkle tinkle trill

One day, the emperor of Japan sent a gift. With it was a letter.

"Great emperor," it began. "I have heard how much you love the song of the nightingale.

"This mechanical bird will sing whenever you wish."

The mechanical nightingale was magnificent: proudly perched and covered in bright jewels. Its song was a delight.

I'll miss you!

trill

"Wonderful," said the emperor. Then he spoke to his daughter. "You can send that dismal grey bird home. We don't need it any more."

The months went by and the emperor
forgot the woodland bird until…

kerplang

The mechanical bird broke.

The emperor was first angry and then sad.

And as the weeks passed without song, he grew sadder.

The emperor's daughter made a plan.

She planted the seed of a tall and twining plant below
a palace window.

Late one summer evening, when the plant's white flowers
were in bloom, the nightingale came back.

Welcome back

treble
treble
trill

25

The Moose and the River

A STORY FROM NORTH AMERICA

Long ago, when the world was new, there was
a beautiful river. The fish swam happily.
Animals came to drink.
   Then the giant moose heard about the river
and came down to the edge.

He began to drink. And he kept on drinking.
Every day, he came to drink.
The days went by and the river grew shallower and
shallower.
The fish were worried. All the animals were worried too.

gurgle slurp

Raccoon tried to scare Moose.

snarrr

yahowl

Wolf tried to scare Moose.

Bear tried to scare Moose.

GRRR

CRASH

And Beaver gnawed a tree so it fell by his tail. Moose didn't even notice.

"I'll make Moose go somewhere else," said Fly.
But the other creatures only jeered.
But Fly just did what he could do.

Zzzz ZZZ ZZZZ

And Moose ran away.
Fly had saved the river.

The Tree and the Reed

A STORY FROM AESOP

The tree held its leaves towards the sun.

"Marvellous," it said. "I can feel myself growing taller and stronger."

It looked down at the grass.

"Are you wilting in the heat?" The grass gave a feeble wave. "I'll be alright."

I'll pick myself up.

The next day, the rain came.
"Very refreshing," said the tree.
"I can feel myself growing taller and
stronger."
It looked down at the grass.
"Are you feeling a bit battered?"
The grass slumped under the
weight of raindrops.
"I'll be alright."

I'll pick myself up.

The day after that, the wind blew hard and it howled its horrid song.

"You can't hurt me," said the tree. "I'm so tall and strong."

It looked down at the grass.

"Are you getting flattened down there?"

The grass could hardly answer as the wind flapped it this way and that.

"I'll be alright."

I'll pick myself up.

Then, without warning…

The tree was blown down. Its branches snapped as they crashed to earth.

Its roots stuck out in the air.

"Oh dear," whispered the grass. "Um… Hello, Tree. Hello! Are you alright?"

For a long, long moment, the tree did not reply.

CRASH

Then it rustled its leaves.

"I… I'm not entirely sure," it said. "There seems to be a problem."

I don't think I can pick myself up.

The Story That Grew

tra la la

BASED ON A STORY FROM BENGAL

Late one afternoon, a farmer was going home from working in the fields. As he walked he sang his favourite little song.

Suddenly he felt something in his mouth. He stopped to pull it out.

That evening, as he was eating supper with his wife, he told the story of how he stopped in the middle of his song.

"And do you know what I found in my mouth?" he said. "A lark feather."

How odd

Really

The next day, the farmer's wife went to market with her neighbour.

"A very odd thing happened yesterday," she told her friend.

"My husband was out in the fields singing, and a lark feather came out of his mouth."

At the market, the neighbour met her sister, who had also come to market.

"My neighbour told me an amazing story," she explained. "Her husband was singing in the fields, and a lark flew out of his mouth."

Astonishing

The sister travelled home to her village with the baker who had brought her wares to market.

She was so taken with the story that she wanted to pass it on.

"My sister's neighbour's husband is a wonderful singer," she said, "and when he sings, larks fly out of his mouth."

And the next day, the baker told all her customers about the marvel she had heard.

Amazing

We must go and see!

Outside in the street, they began to talk to one another.

"The baker's friend's sister's neighbour's husband sings so well that, as soon as he opens his mouth, larks fly out."

"And a blackbird as well, I hear."

"And a song thrush."

The women decided that they must go and see the farmer whose singing made birds fly out of his mouth.

So they took a horse and cart, went to his house, and asked him to perform the marvel.

But all he sang was his favourite little song.

tra la la

"What about the birds?" they wanted to know.

"Birds?" he said. "What birds?"

The Water and the Well

A STORY FROM IRAN

There was once a farmer who had many sheep. The sheep had lambs, and then the farmer had more sheep.

"I am pleased to have so many," he said to himself, "but my pond is too small to provide them with water."

He went to his neighbour.

"You have a well in the field next to mine," he said. "Will you sell it to me so I have water for my sheep?"

The neighbour agreed.

maa

baa

38

The very next day, the farmer put out a trough for his sheep. He took a bucket and went to the well for water.

The neighbour came running up, shaking his fist.

Villain! Thief!

But...

"How dare you steal my water!" he shouted.

"I'm not a thief," said the farmer. "You sold me this well and I paid what you asked."

"I sold you the well," said the neighbour. "I did not sell you the water."

The two men could not agree, so they went and asked a judge to decide.

The judge listened carefully as the farmer explained how and why he had bought the well.

More money

Then the judge turned to the neighbour.

"What is the problem with what this farmer says?" he asked.

"I sold the farmer my well," said the neighbour. "I did not mention the water. My price did not include the water. Taking the water will cost extra."

The judge looked at one man and then at the other. He looked at the ceiling and down at his book.

He closed his eyes and sighed. Then he opened his eyes and leaned forward.

"You sold the well," he said to the neighbour. "And that means you no longer have the right to keep your water in it.

"Either you take your water out, or you pay rent to the farmer for keeping it in his well."

"But while the water remains and you pay no rent, the farmer may treat it as his."

gurgle

41

The King's Highway

A WORLD STORY

The king stood on the palace balcony, beaming with delight. "Messengers have brought good news," he told his chancellor. "I am now king of all the lands around.

"I am going on a journey to visit them all.

"And when I come back, I want to ride in along a great highway paved with marble."

The chancellor looked where the king was pointing.

"Your Majesty," he said. "The highway would run straight through farms and gardens. Look – you can see people hoeing and weeding from here."

"That's a problem for you to solve," said the king. "I will be back in six months."

42

The chancellor had
to do as he was told. He sent messengers to
warn the people that the king needed their land.

Then he sent workers to tear up the farms and gardens and
build the road.

After six months, the road was ready: gleaming marble
pavestones wide enough for the king's procession.

But the king's tour of his lands took longer than expected. News came that he would not be back for another year.

And in that time, the sun shone.

The rain fell.

By the edge of the highway and under the marble paving, seeds began to grow.

And grow.

And grow.

And the people laughed as they gathered armfuls of flowers and baskets of vegetables.

Then the king arrived without warning and summoned the chancellor to his camp outside the city.

"The highway!" he said to his chancellor. "What sort of highway is this! I am the ruler of all the lands around."

"But you see," said the chancellor, "you may think you rule the lands because you rule the people. But you cannot rule the earth itself. Instead of a royal procession, may I suggest a harvest feast."

And the king said yes.

Hurrah!